It worked. Raymond was back in his room.

His mother would kill him if he made a mess of the house. The situation was hopeless.

Raymond knew he had one last chance to save himself. He shouted as loud as he could:

He was falling a thousand feet a second. Right toward his house.

He was going to crash through the roof.

Raymond was ducking missiles in outer space again.

But that wasn't the worst part. The worst part was that his backpack-autopower-vapor-writer had failed.

But nothing happened. Raymond had used up his MEANWHILES…

The mountain lion gulped him down in one bite. Raymond was swallowed alive.

He felt around in his holster for the rusty bullet. It wasn't there. The situation was hopeless.

Raymond knew he had one last chance to save himself. He took off a cowboy boot. With the pointy nail of his big toe, he carved out on the lion's tummy:

Raymond knew he had one last chance to save himself. He dipped his finger into the vial of ink and printed on the side of the ship:

Raymond was out West again.

Raymond was walking
the plank again.

Over he went into
the shark-infested sea.
The situation was hopeless.

The leftover Martians zoomed in on him. The situation was hopeless.

Raymond knew he had one last chance to save himself. He switched on his backpack-autopower-vaporwriter.

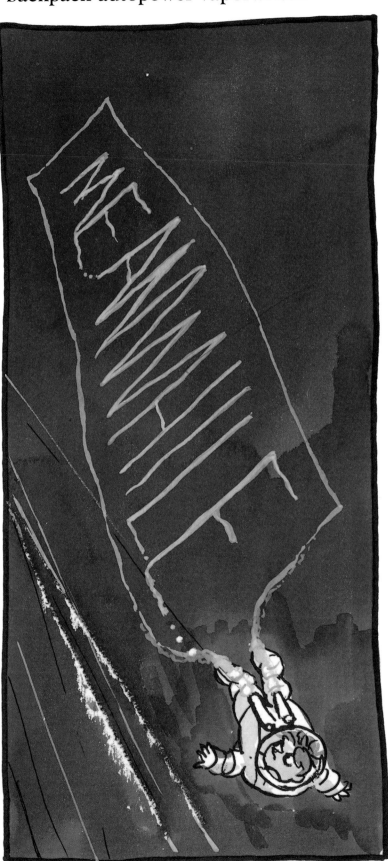

Raymond lost his aft . . .

And then his fore.

He evened the odds against him by shooting down 112 Martian spaceships.

The evil two-headed King of the Martians got in a lucky shot.

Raymond was in outer space, being chased by Martians.

The mountain lion leaped. The situation was hopeless.

Raymond knew he had one last chance to save himself. He made a mad dash over to the nearest rock, and with the pointy end of the rusty bullet he scratched out: MEANWHILE…

Until it was almost too late. He reached for his gun.

He didn't have a gun.

How could he be a cowboy out West and not have a gun?

The only thing he found in his holster was a rusty bullet.

Raymond did not see the ferocious mountain lion . . .

Right into an avalanche!

Lucky for Raymond, he was a great trick rider. He maneuvered his horse to miss the falling rocks.

Raymond tried to reason with the posse.

But the posse couldn't care less. They kept shooting.

Raymond made a sharp left and galloped into a canyon . . .

Raymond was out West, being chased by a posse.

He didn't know why. Maybe because he was wearing a mask and they mistook him for an outlaw.

"Wait!" cried the beautiful maiden.

So right there on the plank, Raymond wrote on the scroll: MEANWHILE…

Raymond knew he had one last chance to save himself.

"It's the law of the sea that I have to grant you your last request," grumbled the Captain, who had a hook and a peg leg and a patch on one eye. And so did the rest of his crew.

But none of the pirates had anything to write with. And why should they? None of them could read.

The only reason he didn't capture the pirate captain was his sword broke.

So Raymond was forced to walk the plank. The situation was hopeless.

Then swung by a rope over the shark-infested sea onto the Royal naval vessel.

He dueled the wicked pirates singlehanded. And also rescued a beautiful maiden.

Wicked pirates were boarding a Royal naval vessel. They were dueling the Queen's loyal sailors.

Raymond couldn't just stand by and watch as if it were a picture in a comic book.

He clenched a sword between his teeth . . .

Raymond was on a pirate ship on the high seas.

Unbelievable! He had MEANWHILED...!

It was a word comics always use to change the scene. MEANWHILE.
But inside a box: MEANWHILE... with three dots after it. And
what it meant was that wherever you were in a story, just a plain,
ordinary MEANWHILE... was going to take you somewhere else.

"What if I had my own MEANWHILE... ?" Raymond wondered.
And with a red marker he scrawled the word on the wall behind
his bed, where he hoped his mother wouldn't see it.

Raymond's mother didn't get to finish her threat.

With Raymond's mother, it was always "Right now!" and never "No big deal, you can do it next Tuesday, Raymond." Suddenly . . .

Raymond's eye caught a word in the middle of the page.

Raymond didn't hear.

Now Raymond heard. It was his mother. She was always finding things for him to do.

"Maybe she'll forget," thought Raymond.

Text and pictures copyright © 1997 by Jules Feiffer
All rights reserved
Library of Congress catalog card number: 97–70129
Printed in the United States of America
Designed by Steve Scott
First edition, 1997

NHILE...

JULES FEIFFER

Michael di Capua Books ▪ HarperCollins Publishers